Mulatto®

Randy R. & Timothy Durham

Published by RC Management and
Publishing Services
Greenvale, NY 11548

ISBN: 9798448776298ISBN
Library of Congress Control Number:
2022906413
Cover designed by Timothy Durham and
enhanced by RC Management and Publishing
Services
Orders by U.S. trade bookstores and
wholesalers please contact us at
http://rcmanagementpa.com
rcmanagementpa@gmail.com

I would like to dedicate this book series
"MULATTO " to my girls Jenna Roller, Nina and
Gia McCarthy especially my Angel in Heaven
Stephanie Kolman Roller also my immediate
family Otis Boyd, Cynthia Roller and family
forever in my heart.
RANDOLPH ROLLER

Contents

Chapter 1

"Back To Business"

Jenina is not enjoying the trip back to the United States because she is unsure if she's pregnant.

She has this feeling inside of her that she's never had before. As they cruise up to the port, they see a police presence as though the police were waiting for someone to return. Tony turns to Jenina says, "Jenina, this day was going to come. I know they're here for me, and I'm just ready to get this over with."

Jenina says, sobbing, "I'm going to miss you."

Tony replies, "It's not going to be for long Jenina, I have things working, so I shouldn't be away for a long time."

He continues, "I felt this day was coming. This is why I asked you in Bermuda if you can handle things while I'm away. I trust no one, only you. Momo and Big Ron will be by your side the whole time. They are very loyal. They've never let me down. You've seen that at the hotel. They are by your side also."

Jenina, still sobbing, gives Tony a big hug and a kiss. He walks down the ramp, and the police place him in handcuffs. Jenina holds back her tears because she knows she has to be strong, especially if she is pregnant. She has a lot of thinking to do and has to muster all the strength she can.

Meanwhile, as Tony's being placed into the police car, he spots officer O'Leary in the crowd of blue, who gives him a wink, letting him know that things are all set and not to worry. His case has already been settled internally at this time. Jenina's mind is a mess. She doesn't know what to do first. She believes the first thing she needs to do is inform Joseph and the crew of what happened to Tony. She gets a cab with all their luggage to Joseph's house.

As the cab turns around the fountain, Jenina heads toward the front door, where Joseph and Stephanie are in the doorway. Jenina sees the look on their face like they know what happened.

Jenina gets out of the cab and approaches them. They reach their arms out for a hug, and they whisper in each other's ear, one to the other, saying, "He's going to be okay."

Jenina immediately asks Stephanie to come into the parlor. She needs to talk to her. As Joseph begins to make phone calls to take care of business, Jenina and Stephanie are in the parlor talking about the future of Tony and Jenina. Stephanie hugs Jenina as she is sobbing.

Stephanie says, "You have to be strong. There are a lot of things that need to be done that Tony is counting on you to do."

Jenina replies, "I understand that, but there's something that I haven't told anyone."

Stephanie says, "What is it? There's nothing that we can't take care of."

Jenina replies, "I believe I'm pregnant."

Stephanie says, "That changes some things, but we can take care of that. First, we have to get you to the doctors. Does Tony know?"

Jenina replies, "I wasn't sure, so I never told him but I'm almost sure."

"I'll set up an appointment for you right away," says Stephanie.

Jenina thanks Stephanie, "Thank you, I really need to know for sure."

Stephanie says reassuringly, "We will go from there and figure how we can fix things, don't worry."

Chapter 2
"Careful Planning"

Stephanie and Jenina are heading to Tony's house with luggage.

Stephanie is going to help Jenina unpack.

Joseph is in a meeting with Momo and Big Ron – they have a lot of planning to do.

Jenina still has a sad look on her face.

Stephanie tells Jenina, "Stop worrying. We can handle this. I've been through this myself before with Joseph. I understand how you feel, but if you feel as though you're having a hard time coping with this. I'm always, always here for you."

Stephanie continues, "You have an appointment. I will take you to the doctor and we'll figure out what we have to do after that."

Jenina replies, "Okay, I trust you. Tony told me this day would come, so I'm kind of happy. Actually, I'm not really happy, but relieved this will all be over soon." She continues, "I also promised Tony that, when this day came, I would be strong for us. I also plan to visit him in jail."

Stephanie replies, "You're probably one of the only people that can go and see him. That is very convenient for us. At least we have some communication with Tony, knowing some of the things that he wants to be done.

Stephanie calls for the car.

Momo picks up Stephanie and Jenina, and they head for the doctors. The conversation in the vehicle is pretty quiet, and then Momo says, "Jenina, Stephanie, whatever you guys need, let me know. I'm here for you. I will lay my life down for Tony, and that goes the same for the both of you."

At this time, Joseph is in the study thinking about preparing what needs to be done to make sure that the structure of the family stays intact while Tony is in jail. His first thoughts are to let Jenina visit Tony and to bring back information that is needed to keep the family together. But he's also thinking what the other Capo's would think - that this is dangerous by letting the family be run by not only a woman but a negro woman. This is an unprecedented move and would most likely get push back from the Association.

He must think long and hard about this, but it seems to be the only answer, being as though no one else, especially from the family, can visit Tony in jail, and this is Tony's crew. At the doctor's, Jenina is very nervous. She has a lot of things going through her head, *"Am I pregnant? How is Tony doing in jail? Is the family going to stay together?"*

Stephanie's trying to keep her calm, but she looks pretty nervous.

The doctor enters the room and looks Jenina in the eyes, and says, "You're pregnant. You must remain calm. I know some of the things you're going through. I spoke with Joseph earlier this morning, but you must remain calm."

Chapter 3

"Securing Allies"

Jenina has so much to think about. The first thing she must do is find out who is on her side and who is against her in the family. She has more to worry about than Momo and Big Ron because of the fact that Tony and Joseph's crew has about 120 men plus four captains, so about thirty men each. She must have a sit down with Joseph and the captains to feel out who is on her side and who will be loyal to Tony and Joseph no matter what they ask of them. Jenina being pregnant, and having this vast responsibility, is unknown to Tony because he doesn't know that she carrying a child. That's why Jenina must have good timing with telling him because she knows that he wouldn't want her to go through any stress. Who else could

Tony actually depend on to do what needs to be done?

Jenina wants to talk to Stephanie to see if she has any answers, so she doesn't make any mistakes. So Jenina goes to Scalia's home to talk to Stephanie.

They went to the Parlor and shut the door.

Jenina asks Stephanie, "What should I do?"

The first thing Stephanie says is, "Find out if Tony is being extradited to Florida to stand trial for the death of Salvatore Calabrese. Don't tell Tony about the pregnancy before he gets sent to Florida, since you're newly pregnant."

Stephanie believes the timing of Tony hopefully getting out and her having a baby should be fairly close.

Jenina also asks Stephanie about the meeting with Tony and the crew captains, and Stephanie thinks it's a great idea. This way, they can feel out who is on Jenina's side and who would be a problem.

To make sure everything is done the right way, they decide to do one thing at a time.

Stephanie tells Jenina, "I will take care of setting up the meeting with Joseph and the captains and they will go from there. Absolutely no one is to know about the pregnancy. Knowing that this is Tony's child may spark some criticism from the crew."

Stephanie cooks dinner and feels as though this is a great time to talk to Joseph and Jenina together. Jenina desperately wants to honestly know who is on her side before she takes on this huge responsibility.

Chapter 4

"Completing The Puzzle"

As the three of them finish eating dinner, Stephanie speaks up about the meeting with Tony and Joseph's captains.

Stephanie says, "Joseph, in order to pull this off we must have complete and utter cooperation from the crew."

Joseph replies, "You're right. We must let everyone know about Jenina's position in our crew and must be on board 100% with what we're doing because the bottom line is to keep our position in the family. We must never look weak because Tony is in jail. I will set up a meeting, and whoever is not with us will be dealt with accordingly. We'll get this all straightened out so we can move on and get Tony back home as soon as possible." He turns to Jenina, "But until then, I have our lawyer who's going to come and take you to see Tony for the first time. To make sure you are protected, Momo and Big Ron will go with you on the ride."

Jenina, being nice and full, told the Scala's that she's going to Tony's house, which is actually hers also. She needs to get a good night's sleep for the trip tomorrow to the county jail where Tony is being held until the trial date.

Sleeping in bed without being next to Tony is a strange and unsettling feeling to her, but from all the confusion and tiredness, she finally falls fast asleep. At six o'clock in the morning, Jenina's alarm goes off. She wakes up in excitement to see Tony today. However, Jenina is feeling sick this morning, but she knows that this is very important, and she can't miss this meeting, so she gathers up the clothes she's wearing, and she gets ready to doll herself up. Around ten after seven, Jenina hears a knock at the door.

It's Stephanie.

Stephanie says, "Good morning, princess."

Jenina gives her a hug and says, "Good morning."

Stephanie says, "How are you feeling this morning?"

Jenina replies, "Not too well but really excited to see Tony. It's been a couple of days, and I miss him so much."

Stephanie says, "I understand fully. It's happened to me a couple of times with Joseph. It'll be fine. It's just part of the business. So, let's do what we have to do today to get things rolling. Joseph got word that Tony will be extradited to Florida, which makes it a lot easier for us. The trial will be in Florida."

Jenina replies, "That's what Tony always said, that it would be easier for us if it was in Florida, so it's a blessing. He's not a bad guy. I noticed that he only acts when he's being threatened, or his family is being threatened."

Stephanie replies, "Yes, that we know. He's not really a bad guy, he just protects his own. Okay, let's get a move on."

Big Ron and Momo are waiting in the car at the house, so they both head for the car and are on their way.

Chapter 5

"A Visit to The Tombs"

'The Tombs' is a colloquial name for the Manhattan Detention Complex in Lower Manhattan where Tony is being held. It is located at one hundred and twenty-five White Street in Lower Manhattan.

When they arrive, the only one allowed to see Tony is Jenina. In spite of all of the illegal and demeaning body searches done to her to even step foot into the jail, nothing will stop her from seeing Tony. She misses him very much. Just to get to see his face will bring joy to her heart and knowing that he is okay. This is a sad place, poorly lit, very dull, with a foul stench and a sense of chaos in the air. There are people everywhere: yelling, screaming, and barking orders. This is making Jenina's head spin.

The worst for her was waiting in line seeing all of these things happen. It's something she never thought she'd have to endure. But then again, to see Tony, she'd go through anything.

The line she had to wait in was long and grueling. After a lengthy wait, Jenina finally gets to see Tony. Her eyes light up. It doesn't feel right for her not to give him a hug and kiss.

She says to Tony, concerned, "How are you feeling? Are you okay?"

Tony replies, "I'm doing fine. I have a lot of friends in here, Jenina. Don't worry. How are you? You're looking great."

Jenina says, "I'm okay, but it's tough out here without you. Thank God for Stephanie and Joseph. Without them I think I would have fallen apart." Jenina says softly, "I love you, Tony."

Tony replies, "I love you too, Jenina. We don't have much time for what we spoke about earlier. I must ask you to go to Joseph and tell him I said that, along with Big Ron and Momo, you must help run this crew until Vincent figures out how to get me out of here."

Jenina replies, "What makes you think that they would listen to a woman? Especially a black woman?"

Tony replies, "It doesn't matter what they think. If they want to be in my crew, they have to listen to you. You're the only one between myself and them, so you must be strong. I need you to be strong. It's not going to be easy. You need to find out who's on my side. Even though the Calabrese crew are pretty much out of the way, you have to look out for Chicago. Here inside, I got word that Chicago is going to try to take over. That's why I said you must be strong. I know you can do it. The Calabrese crew territory is wide open. They're going to try to snatch it.

"I know how smart you are, Jenina. You can outsmart them. Just be careful. You have all the backup you need. Do whatever you have to do to keep this crew together. Joseph will handle letting them know what's going on.

"Also, I need you to see me weekly so I can tell you what needs to be done until I get out of here.

"Here comes the turnkey. Our time is over. I love you so much, Jenina. Please be careful and have a meeting with Momo and Big Ron to figure out who is against this move in the crew that I'm putting you in charge of."

Jenina says, softly, "Tony, I will do the best I can. You know I have your best interest at heart."

Tony replies, "Just know you're the only one I can really depend on. I love you."

Jenina replies as she's being escorted out, "I love you too."

As Jenina is leaving the jailhouse, she's feeling bad because Tony doesn't know that she's pregnant and he's putting a lot of pressure on her. But she's feeling as any woman would feel, that she has to protect her own, and she'll do whatever she has to do to get the job done.

Chapter 6

"Strategic Thinking"

As Jenina heads to the car, she has this feeling of something inside, making her feel strong to do what she has to until Tony gets out. On top of her pregnancy, she has a crew to run and also has a possible nemesis in Chicago. What bothers her the most is if Tony knew that he was putting her and their child in danger, he would somehow break out of there. He has the influence and money to get that done, but she doesn't want him to go that route. She wants him to trust the process so that when he's done with this case, he will be truly free.

What she needs to do as soon as possible is to have a sit down with Joseph, Momo, and Big Ron. She needs Joseph to be there. This is her first meeting about the subject. Joseph will need to help Jenina, so she doesn't say anything to them on the way back to the house.

She's going to have to wait until she speaks with Joseph first, then she's going to set up the meeting. These first couple of days are very crucial.

When she gets in the car, Stephanie asks, "How is Tony, Jenina?"

Jenina replies, "As well as he can be. He told me he has a few allies inside, so he has some people to watch over him while he's there." Stephanie tells Jenina, "This is the best thing, to just get it done and over with. He'll be fine."

She replies, "I know he's going to be fine. I am just sad because I can't share the good news with him right now."

Stephanie says, "In due time, when the time is right. Let's just get you home and get you a nice hot bath, good food, and let you relax. You had a very grueling day."

Chapter 7

"Unlikely Visit"

Olivia Calabrese, twenty-seven, fair skin, red head, is one of the top dancers at the club and also Frank Calabrese's daughter. On a typical night, she can have any guy she wants. All the guys want her, except for Tony, who has his heart set on Jenina. This pisses Olivia off and makes her want him even more.

At the club, Olivia sits in her dressing room, digging her manicured nails into her head, infuriated. She says to the club owner, "How dare a black woman take Tony away from me? He is probably sitting in his cell all hot and heavy. I'm going to show him what he's missing." She continues, "I've been waiting for my chance."

Olivia knows that Tony and Jenina are together, but she thinks Tony can do way better. She hails a cab and says to the driver, "Manhattan Detention Complex, Lower Manhattan."

In the cab, she grabs a tiny black dress out of her bag and puts it on. Even though she wants to, she knows she can't go into the detention center in her bra and panties. She still has her six-inch black pump heels on.

In the cab, she fantasizes about Tony and is thinking about how she wants to get him alone and wear nothing but heels for him. Like a model, Olivia struts through the hallways like it's nobody's business. The guards let her through because she kissed one of them on the cheek. Tony is told by the guards to wait in the recreational room. He has a visitor.

Tony's mind is racing, "Who the hell is coming here? What do they want? I only want to see Jenina."

Olivia's eyes lock with Tony's as soon as she sees him. Tony immediately looks away. Gritting his teeth, he says quietly, "What the hell are you doing here, Olivia?"

Olivia eyes Tony up from the top of his head down to the tips of his toes. She is fantasizing about taking that orange jumpsuit off and having her way with him. As she's gripping her thighs, she says seductively, "Tony, I want you so badly. I thought about you the entire ride here. I had a dream about you last night. I must have you."

"Olivia, you know I only have eyes for Jenina. It was love at first sight with her. I haven't thought about you for one second," Tony says, straight as an arrow.

Olivia tries to playfully touch Tony's chest. The guard immediately catches her and yells, "No touching. If you try that again, you are out of here."

Olivia immediately pulls back. "You know, Tony, I thought long and hard about this. Why don't you and I run away together? We can leave as soon as you get out. Just you and me," says Olivia.

Tony replies, "Liv, are you literally insane? Insane in the brain? I am going to be with Jenina for the rest of my life."

"Not if I have something to do with it," snaps Olivia.

"You stay away from Jenina," yells Tony. He continues, "Do not touch her, look at her, go anywhere near her. Hell, don't even smell her. Jenina is my queen. She is the reason I get up every single morning. You will never, ever mean that much to me."

Olivia is getting pissed. "Oh, so you like black women.. hmm? Does chocolate spice up your life Tony? I heard she doesn't even know who her real Daddy is. What a shame."

Tony is shaking. Tony gets up out of his chair. He turns around, looks at her, and says,

"She may not know who he is, but I do. He's a very important man, just as your dad was." Tony turns back around and walks away towards the guard and says, "Take me back to my cell."

As he's walking away, she replies, "My dad was an important man too, and if it takes my last breath, I will find out who murdered him. That fire at his warehouse was done on purpose. Do you have anything to say about that, Tony?"

Tony looks at her one more time and says, "Stay away from her. I really mean it."

This conversation Olivia just had with Tony didn't get her anywhere. It only made the situation worse. She is fuming mad, her face turning as red as her hair. As she's gracefully walking away, she mumbles to herself, "We'll see."

Chapter 8

"Meeting Minutes"

As Jenina and the crew return home, she approaches Joseph and gives him a big hug. He asked, "How did it go?"

Jenina replies, "It went fine. He's doing okay. Tony has a few friends in there and is just awaiting his extradition. He gave me specific instructions. We must sit down with Momo and Big Ron. I need to ask them to do a few things."

Stephanie says, "We have plenty of time for that. Right now, I'm going to cook a good meal so that you guys can eat."

Joseph replies, "Good idea. Jenina, let's go to the parlor. I want to talk to you alone."

Joseph and Jenina walk to the parlor and shut the door. Joseph says, "I need to ask you-"

Jenina interrupts, "Okay, I understand. I know where this is going."

Joseph replies, "Then you know that we have a big problem. We have to be careful with what we do and who we do it with. If the word gets out to the Association, we're all in trouble. We need to talk to Big Ron and Momo and see how they feel about getting this done behind the scenes. I already have trust in them." Joseph continues, "Okay. I had the feeling that Anthony really has a lot of trust in you, and so do I, but the other crew members might be a little upset about how this thing is going. I know you have the knowledge and the skill to get things done. The thing is, if we keep this under wraps, the other gangs will never believe that you're running this crew. They will think that it's me. I'm too old to make decisions like this. You're young, thoughtful, and skillful, as I mentioned before, but the best thing you have going for you is your love for Anthony. After dinner, you, Momo, Big Ron, and I will come back to this parlor and strategize. For right now, let's get cleaned up and we will eat dinner, have a couple of drinks and figure this thing out."

Jenina gives him a big hug and heads to the bathroom to get cleaned up and ready for dinner.

Chapter 9

"Cacio e pepe" / "Chicago"

The aroma of the pasta wafts through Stephanie and Joseph's lovely home.

Momo says, "It smells like Italy's capital, Rome. I've been there once, on some business. I had the best cacio e pepe you have ever tasted..."

Joseph laughs, "Ha. Then you haven't had Stephanie's pasta. Stephanie, is everything ready?"

She replies, "Yes I set the table for myself, you, Big Ron, Momo, and Jenina. Have a seat."

Everyone gathers around the table. Stephanie brings out the first two courses. First red wine, then a homemade Italian salad with rosemary bread.

Jenina makes a toast, "I would like to make a toast to Momo and Big Ron. Thank you for guiding me and protecting my family. Same with you Stephanie and Joseph, I can always count on you guys. Thank you for welcoming me into your home and for this delicious meal. And cheers to Tony, I miss you baby. Cheers everyone."

They are laughing, making jokes, having high spirits. Stephanie brings out her homemade cacio e pepe, garnished with black pepper, Pecorino-Romano cheese and extra-virgin olive oil. She also brings out the meatballs.

"Wow, Stephanie, those are the largest meatballs I have ever seen."

Stephanie replies, "Buon appetite, especially you, Momo. I hope you like the pasta."

Momo and Big Ron eat three plates of Stephanie's homemade cacio de pepe. Jenina eats two.

Momo says with a mouthful, "Stephanie, next time, I will just come over here instead of going to Italy. This is the best pasta I have ever tasted."

Stephanie says with a smile, "You are welcome anytime. Why don't you all gather in the parlor? I will bring you some dessert wine. I know you have some business to take care of."

Each with a dessert wine in hand, Joseph, Big Ron, Momo, and Jenina gather in the parlor.

Jenina says, "Alright, let's talk business."

Joseph takes the floor. The first thing he says is, "This conversation does not leave this room. This is between us. We are the only hope of this crew making it." He continues about Tony, "I've already contacted our lawyers in Florida about getting him out of jail. They're setting things up to get him the least time possible because it is an open and closed case of involuntary manslaughter.

"However, we have a few things we have to do. Number one, Jenina is calling the shots from now on. She will come to me for guidance on exactly what needs to be done. But Jenina is going to make her own strategy. The threat we have in Chicago has to be eliminated.

"Once we show our strength, we can back off and concentrate on our business. We've lost a lot of money. We can't have any more of that. On that note, does anyone else have anything more to say?"

Momo answers, "You remember Nico, from the club? He told me that one of our crew's captains is talking negative about Jenina. We can't have that. Nico also said to me that this crew captain is sleeping with Olivia, Frank Calabrese's daughter."

Joseph says, "I understand, that will be dealt with, but Chicago first. Jenina, what's your take on the Chicago thing?"

Jenina replies, "Well, since we can't kill a boss, we have to do something really drastic." She exclaims, "I have an idea! We must go there on our own. We can't kill him when we can take out some of this crew."

Joseph says, "That's going to be dangerous. Do you know or do you think you know how you can get this done?"

She replies, "I have an idea and I believe it would work. It's dangerous but it has to be done. Most of his crew is here in New York because they are planning a takeover, but we don't know where. That also means the boss is pretty much alone in Chicago, weak. That gives us an advantage. It's almost a one-day train ride to Chicago. We could get there, do what we have to do, and come back in the next 24 hours. So, I'm planning on being away for two days.

"In the meantime, please have Stephanie contact my family and make sure everything's okay. I'm quite sure it is but I just have to make sure. Just like I explained to Tony, I'm going to do what I have to do to get this done."

Chapter 10

"Three Train Tickets, Please"

After this meeting with the boys, Jenina clearly knows that she has to do something extreme, something that would gain her respect from the crew. She's clearly upset finding out that Armand, one of the captains in the crew, is talking behind their backs about her pulling the strings for the crew. Something must be done before he becomes a cancer in the crew, starts to spread, and she loses some of the men to this rebellion.

She has her rumors about Armand Tucci sleeping with Frank Calabrese's daughter, Olivia. Olivia is clearly the nemesis of her. Jenina must put a stop to this because she believes Armand is leaking information to Olivia.

Also, Olivia was always against Jenina at the club. Jenina knows where this is coming from, it is obviously that Olivia's always had a thing for Tony. Tony really doesn't like her, especially because she's the daughter of Frank Calabrese. But Jenina is running out of time. She has no time for this. She has to gather her thoughts and figure out a way to get the Chicago thing under control on her own.

One thing that's bothering her is the safety of her family. She hasn't spoken to them in such a long time. Jenina knows they're safe because Trigger would never let anything happen to them.

First, she needs to figure out what they're going to do about the boss in Chicago. Jenina decides that Big Ron, Momo, and her are going to go to Chicago on a twenty-hour ride to do this thing themselves. She instructs Momo to get three tickets both ways to Chicago.

This is going to be the most insane thing that she has ever done. It's worth it to Jenina because if she pulls this off, she will get the respect she needs from the crew. It's kind of dangerous because she is pregnant. She knows she still must be careful before she leaves. She needs Stephanie to get in touch with her. Family is so important to her.

As the sun is rising, Joseph packs the car with the minimal bags they have, an outfit for everyone, just in case. He wants Big Ron,

Momo, and especially Jenina to rest as much as they can.

Joseph opens the blinds, one by one, waking them up. Stephanie makes a quick breakfast, calico pepper frittatas with red and green peppers. Big Ron starts the car. Momo hops in the front. Jenina lays in the back with a plastic bag with morning sickness. Big Ron and Momo don't know she's pregnant, she plays it off like it was Stephanie's frittata.

They arrive at the train station. Big Ron and Momo help get Jenina to the train. They have a long ride ahead of them.

As they arrive in Chicago, they approach the hotel that the boss owns. There is a feeling of anxiety that Jenina feels but she knows she has the protection of Momo and big Ron. The hotel is heavily guarded by his men this was expected so the plan that they hatched in New York can go just as planned. Big Ron acts like he is a customer. He goes inside and he chokes out the 1st guard inside the lobby. Then Momo comes in behind him as Jenina holds back.

On the way up the 3rd floor, Momo and big Ron silently take out the guards one floor at a time
until they reached the office and Momo knocks on the door.

The boss says, without knowing who it is, "Come in!"

He busts the door in and startles the boss.

"Who the hell are you and what are you doing in my hotel?" says the boss.

Momo replies by put both hands on the table.

"Where are my guards?" sputters the boss.

Momo says, "You don't have to worry about them anymore! I want to introduce you to someone."

Jenina graciously enters the room the boss says, "If I'm not mistaken, you're the Negro woman that everyone acts like they're scared of. But I'm not scared of you!"

Jenina replies, "You should be, because greetings from New York, but your men are no longer here to protect you! So, keep your hands on the desk where I can see them, we need to have a conversation. Listen! I know you're trying to take the territory of the Calibrese family that's not gonna happen as long as I'm alive, Tony and Joseph are alive, you'll never get it. So, pull your man out of New York or do you see these photos?" Jenina throws photos of his family on his desk and says, "If you don't pull your men out of New York your family will never be the same when I get done with them."

He replies, "Where did you get these pictures? Don't harm my family!"

"If you do what you're supposed to do, then I won't. But if you don't they're all dead and so are you!" Jenina reaches inside of her shawl and pulls out a Tommy gun. She clicks it and says to him, "I mean business. So, if you're smart, you'll do what I'm telling you to do and stay out of New York. New York belongs to the Scalia family and the association."

Jenina puts the Tommy gun back in her shawl, holding onto it as she turns around. She hears a noise. She turns her back to the boss. He's reaching under the desk, and he pulls out a gun. Jenina sees this happen She turns back around and shoots the boss in the chest.

Momo and Big Ron come running in the office Momo says, "This could be trouble big trouble. Let's go! Let's get out of here! Come on now, Jenina! Let's get back to New York. It's OK you did what you had to do."

****

Meanwhile, at the club, Olivia is headlining tonight. A few guys from the crew are there including Nico, Armand, and Domenic Rossi, a newer member. Olivia's wearing a sheer white authentic
lingerie set, a little classier than usual. This was her night. Since he works at the club, Nico's rule for himself is to never hook up with the dancers. Not Armand's. He loves a red-headed, sexy,
strong woman.

Olivia knows she has to work fast. She has to gather all the information she can get from Armand. The way she believes is best is to pretty much seduce him for information because she knows
that Armand is pretty much a whore-monger. But it doesn't matter to her. She feels as though she's on her own ever since her father got murdered. There's no one watching over her anymore.

When her dancing number was over, she asked Nico to whisper into Armand's ear to meet her in the dressing room.

She hears a knock at the door. As she opens the door, she sees it's Armand,
who says, "What's goin' on cutie?"

She grabs him by the wrist, pulls him into the room, and closes the door. Olivia pushes herself very close to him and whispers slowly in his ear, "I know you want me, Armand. I saw you watching me with lust in your eyes." She starts nibbling on his ear and says, "I need a big strong man like you. Can we be friends?"

Armand responds nervously, "Absolutely doll." She starts kissing him and rubbing on his leg, inching closer and closer to his thigh. As his excitement grows, so does another part of his anatomy. She gently strokes it, slowly moving her hand down his pants.

Panting, Olivia says, "If you want to take this any further you must meet me at my apartment tonight after the show."

Armand anxiously replies, "I've always wanted you Olivia, but you're the daughter of a very powerful man."

She says, "I understand, but now he's gone. I need another powerful man to take his place, I choose you baby." She takes her hand out of his pants, zips his zipper and buttons his buttons. Armand enjoys this service.

She says, "9:30 my place and I will show you why I need you so much."

Armand replies, "I wouldn't miss it for the world. I will see you then angel."

After Armand leaves her dressing room she sits down in front of the mirror, looks at herself and she says, "What am I doing? If Tony ever found out about this, he would have us both killed. But me getting revenge on that bitch means more to me than anything. I'm going to destroy her.

Chapter 11

"The Visit"

Harlem, NY in the 1920's. By this time, artistic and cultural expression surrounded the streets.

This period was known as the Harlem Renaissance. Also known as "America's Paris", African American Residents began to replace the Jewish and Italian Americans. This period fostered a new black cultural identity. Duke Ellington's "jungle music" flooded Trigger's home. Jenina's parents and sister have been staying here for months. Trigger's home is safe, or else Jenina's father wouldn't have taken his family here. Jenina's mother knows she is safe but does not like staying in this home. Trigger is a drug dealer. He is the head of the Harlem Mob. People are in and out of the house. She thinks to herself, *"How do I know if one of these men aren't after Trigger?"*

Because of the incident with the Calabrese family, she can't trust anyone. Her mind is in a constant state of worry. Jenina unexpectedly walks through the door, "Hi family." To break away from some of the madness that she's going through, Jenina decided to take a day trip to Harlem to see her family.

Jenina was ecstatic to finally see her family safe and sound in Triggers home. She knows her mother doesn't like being there but it's the safest place for them to be at this time. As she enters the home, she gives her family big hugs and there are smiles all around. Her sister is especially happy to see her.

Her dad says, "My baby girl is finally here. You had us worried with all the trouble that's going on out there. How's Tony doing?"

Jenina replies, "He's doing as well as he could be. He's waiting to be extradited to Florida to get this mess cleared up." She looks at her mom and says, "Mom, I need to talk to you."

Jenina's mom says, "Anything you need baby, I would love to talk to you." Jenina's mom asks, "Would you like something to eat or drink?"

She says, "Not right now, I'm okay. Is there somewhere we can talk? There's something on my mind that I need to talk to you about."

Her mom replies, "Let's go out back, there's no one there and it's really nice outside. We can sit and talk."

The ladies go out back. Jenina gives her mom a big hug and says, "Mom, there's something that I must do and you have to help me with this. I need to see my father."

Her mom replies, "No way Jenina. He's only going to mess your life up. Why should you even want to see him?"

Jenina replies, "I must see him because there's a void in my life. I know who my dad is but I need to know who my father is. With her eyes bellowing up with tears she says, "Mom please help me, I need to know."

Jenina's mom gives her a giant hug and says, "Honey, if you really need to know, ask Tony's father, Joseph. Your father works for him in the garment district. Yes, he is a mobster. I didn't want to tell you before but that's the truth. His name is John Anderson. Just ask Joseph about him and he'll point you in the right direction. Good luck, Jenina. Don't let him hurt you mentally because you do not need that in your life. You're taking on enough. If he hurts you in any way, I will end him, Jenina!"

Jenina hugs her mom and says, "Thank you so much, Mom. I will let you know how things turn out after I get this out of my system.

That way, I won't worry about it anymore. I can move forward with my life."

Her mom says, "Now can I make you guys something to eat? Come back into the house, at least we can have a little family dinner together. We haven't had in a long time your dad would really love that, and your sister also."

Jenina replies, "Okay Mom. Thank you, I love you."

Chapter 12

"Unknown Enemy"

As Jenina and her mother come in from outside. Jenina sees Trigger with his girlfriend and tells them both "Thank you so much for housing my family and keeping them safe."

Trigger replies, "You are welcome sweetheart. I would do anything for this man. This man saved my life and I owe my life to him. Anytime he or any of your family need anything I'm here for you all. I also have armed guards out front protecting your car because in this neighborhood, an Italian man sitting in a car is very suspicious. My guards being outside means no one will ever mess with him. They know he's here for me."

Jenina says, Thank you." She turns to her mother and says, "Mom I can't be long I have Momo in the car waiting for me."

She replies, "Well at least take this plate with you. You haven't had any of my cooking in the longest time."

With that Jenina chuckles. She hugs her mom, sister, and Dad and starts heading for the front door. She says to them, "Thanks everybody. I will see you guys soon. I love you."

Her dad replies, "Stay in touch and stay out of trouble Jenina."

Jenina says, "As soon as this is all over, we will be just fine."

During the ride home, Jenina is talking with Momo. She asks Momo, "Momo, tell me everything you know about John Anderson."

He replies, "I know him he's an arrogant son of a bitch."

Jenina just chuckles and leaves it alone.

Momo continues, "Why are you so concerned about John?"

Jenina replies with a simple, "Just asking" and they head for home. Her stomach is also starting to show a little bit. She needs to work fast. Jenina has no clue what the complications from the pregnancy may be. But she's not afraid. She's grown to be so strong that nothing matters to her except for clearing

all this stuff up so her and Anthony can have a normal life. What she doesn't know is there is an enemy lurking out there that's plotting her downfall.

Her name is Olivia, who in fact has Armand Tucci coming to her apartment tonight to complete his seduction. She is doing this so she can get inside information on Jenina's whereabouts. Olivia is living at Madison Avenue and West 46th Street at the Ritz Carlton Hotel. She is living off her daddy's money he made during prohibition. The only reason why Olivia dances is because she loves it, and she loves the attention. She could easily own her own club, but she doesn't want to put in the work. She can live lavishly the rest of her life off what her dad made. She hears a knock at her door. Looking through the peephole, she sees the man she can't wait to seduce, Armand Tucci. She answers the door in very sleek but elegant nightwear.

Armand's eyes pop out of his head as soon as she opens the door. That red curly hair and her body look so beautiful. Olivia thinks to herself, *"This is going to be a piece ofcake."*

Olivia says to Armand, "Come in and make yourself comfortable." She points to the left, "Over there is a mini bar, make yourself a drink. I'll be right back."

This is all a game to her, and she loves it. This is something that's putting excitement into a little rich girl's head. The thought of being able to seduce someone into doing what she wants them to do is what she really likes. She

likes the power, just like her daddy. While sitting in a chair with a drink in his hand, Armand tries to calm his nerves. He thinks to himself, *"Why am I here? How can I be in the presence of such a rich, beautiful, and damn seductive woman? She is just so powerful to me. I'm just a second*
lieutenant in Joseph army."

None of this is making sense to Armand, but before he can get any other thoughts out of his head. He hears her call him into the bedroom. Still nervous, he gets up out of the chair and walks toward her. As he gets to the bedroom he looks inside and sees this beautiful woman with red hair and big blue eyes sprawled across the bed, an unbelievable sight. He has never seen anything like that, not even in a magazine.

She calls him over to the bed. She unties his tie, unbuttons his shirt, unbuckles his pants. She strips him down and tells him to get on the bed.

The entire time Armand is literally shaking because he feels as though he doesn't even deserve to be there. Women like her only belong to bosses, so he doesn't understand why she's not with one. He thinks, *"Is this luck? Is this fate?"* He's so confused.

She says to him, "What we did at the club was just a prelude to what's about to come."

She lays him on his back. Olivia is totally nude and now so is he. She straddles him like a horse. Armand doesn't say a word. She starts kissing him and she starts to kiss down his chest. Her head goes under the covers. She begins to perform fellatio on him. Armand is completely out of his mind, it's like a dream to him.

After a few minutes of that (which seemed like a lifetime to Armand) she brings her head back from under the covers and then she begins stroking him. She whispers in his ear, "Do not ever tell

anyone about this. I will deny it and it will never happen again."

Armand with his eyes almost in tears replies, "Never will anyone ever know about this. This is somewhat a dream of mine. I love watching you dance so beautifully. I will never mess this up, ever." Olivia put him inside her warm wet pulsating body. Armand is out of his mind while she takes complete control. Olivia is in motion and very aggressive. From her being such a great dancer, positions he could never dream of were no problem for her. She put everything she knew on him. She just gave Armand the time of his life.

As the session winds down, they start to have small pillow talk. Eventually, Jenina comes up in their conversation. Armand states that he knows a little bit about what's going on. He talked to Olivia about the meeting they had and that Jenina was calling the shots for Tony, but he doesn't know much about everything going on with her.

Olivia is satisfied and happy with his response. It's just a start. She knows he hears inside information, so what she did was the right thing. He also mentioned Chicago. But he doesn't know it's already taken care of. He's really rattling off to her, it's exactly what she wanted - to take a chance with someone like Armand and doing what she's doing. She really, really wants to destroy Jenina.

This situation could ruin Olivia. If anyone ever finds out what she did with a low-level crew member. Her father is turning over in his grave and she knows it, but she wants this information so bad that she's willing to risk it all just to destroy Jenina.

Chapter 13

"Biologically Speaking"

As Jenina reaches the house she has one thing in mind and that's meeting her real father. She wants Joseph to call him in from the fashion district to meet, then she's going to speak with him. As she enters the home, she sees Joseph and Stephanie sitting in the parlor.

She walks in and asks, "How's everyone doing?"

They both say together, "Okay and you?"

Jenina replies, "I'm doing fine...Joseph can I speak with you for one second?"

Stephanie gets out of her chair and says, "No problem I'll talk to you guys soon."

Stephanie leaves and closes the door.

Jenina looks at Joseph directly in the eyes and says, "Joseph, you must do me a favor. I need to clear my head of something."

Joseph says, "Anything, what do you need?"

Jenina says, "I know who my biological father is. He is one of your crew members that works in the fashion district. Can you do me a favor and call him in to speak with you?"

Joseph asks, wide-eyed, "Who? Who is that? I know your father is Italian, but I didn't know he was in my crew."

Jenina says, "It's John Anderson."

Joseph's eyes lit up and says, "No way. How can a sweet young lady like you be a spawn of such an evil bastard?"

Jenina replies, "You know, that's funny. Momo said the same thing. Both of you are right."

Joseph says, "He's been a pain in my ass since we've been working together. He does things well, but he doesn't treat his employees the way that they should be treated and that I don't like. The only reason we keep him on is because he's a good earner.

"Listen, I'll get him in here, but when I do, you take it from there. Your father and I don't have much of a rapport together, so I'll have Momo give him a call and get him in here ASAP. For now, young lady, go get something to eat. Stephanie made a beautiful lasagna for dinner tonight. Get Momo in here too."

Jenina gives Joseph a big hug and kiss on the cheek, then walks to the kitchen where Stephanie was standing.

Jenina hugs Stephanie hard and she says, "I'm going to meet my real father and clear my head of all of these thoughts."

"Oh I understand my child," Stephanie replies. "Sometimes some things are best left alone, but it's your choice."

Stephanie looks Jenina in the eye. "I have seen situations like this go south real fast so be careful."

Jenina sits down to a nice plate of lasagna with salad. Jenina, Joseph, Stephanie, and Momo sit around the dining room table having a good time. They are relaxing, talking, and drinking coffee.

Afterwards, the doorbell rings. It's John Anderson. He comes in, gives his greetings and salutations to the family and then Joseph asks him to come into the parlor.

As they're going to the parlor, Joseph says to him, "I don't need to speak with you. Someone else does."

As Joseph walks out, Jenina walks in without saying a word and closes the door.

John's eyes light up and he says, "What is this? Some type of present from Joseph for

being a good boy?"

Jenina replies, "No this was a present 23 years ago."

John says, "What do you mean?"

Jenina says to him, "Take a good look at me."

John pauses for a moment and he says, "No way. No freaking way."

She says, "Yes I am your daughter."

John says, "But how?"

She says, "Do you remember a woman that worked for you named Eloise Lewis?"

John thinks back but he's so old and 23 years is a long time for him to remember. He has destroyed so many other black women's but as he thinks back, he goes, "Oh my God."

Jenina replies, "I am your daughter. Take a good look at the two of us in this mirror. The only thing my mother gave me was her color and her strength and the color is very slight. I look exactly like you."

At this time John is very flush in the face. He can't understand and he doesn't know how she connects with Joseph but he's beginning to feel afraid.

John says, "I said it while she was at the job. I am very sorry if this is my child. I didn't know what else to say."

Jenina firmly says, "I don't want your apology! I just want the reason why."

John says quietly, "She was so beautiful I couldn't resist myself and I was sick in the head with power, but I am a better man today. I just feel so lucky that I met her. I have two children of my own. I loved her."

Jenina replies, "But it was against her will. She only did it because she needed a job because my dad - my REAL dad - couldn't work. She had no choice, and you knew it. You took advantage of her."

"I know. I'm so sorry," John replies. "Do not say you are sorry to me. If it wasn't for you, I wouldn't be here right now so I can't be mad at you. It must have been God's will, but I'm just upset for my mother because you tortured her for months. She loves her husband. She knew it was so wrong for you to do that to her. It has scarred her husband's heart forever. You don't have to worry about Joseph taking any action against you because he knows you're my father and it would hurt me just remember this name for the rest of your life, Jenina Gia Lewis."

John replies, "Wait a second, you said Jenina? You are a legend. You're Anthony's girl, aren't you?"

Jenina replies, "No. I am Anthony's fiancé. Guess what? You don't have to worry about him either. He knows the whole story. I came here because I just needed to clear my head of things. I don't ever want to see you again. Thanks for giving me life but I don't need you in my life. I have a father. Goodbye."

John got his hat and coat and. Joseph escorted him out of the house. Jenina exhaled loudly. Now she can move on.

Chapter 14

"Pushing Forward"

Jenina's swallowing hard after what just happened between her and her father. She remains in the parlor alone for a few minutes before Joseph knocks and enters the parlor.

Joseph asks, "Are you okay, Jenina?"

She replies, "Yes I'm fine."

Joseph asks again, "Is there anything I can do for you? Anything I

can get you?"

She replies, "I'm fine, I'm okay."

Joseph says, "Well I just received some news from Officer O'Leary. You're not going to like it. First thing is this: his men cannot find the gang from Chicago,so he told him they are no longer a threat to the family because the head has been severed from the snake so he paid him off and said this is from Tony. Number two: Armand Tucci has been seen leaving Olivia Calabrese's hotel more than once."

Jenina replies, "Really? That girl never liked me since I've been at the club. She always had something negative to say about me, when mostly everyone else loves me. I never understood why...I think it's because of Anthony."

Joseph says, "I think this is something we can't take lightly. We must look into this Jenina. If he says anything to her that would jeopardize this family's future, it could be devastating, especially if she runs her mouth to the Association about her Biological father. She could be trying to find out the truth about the warehouse fire and the death of her father since Armand was in on it. That could be very dangerous to us. We have to bring him in as soon as possible."

Jenina needs to make an executive decision immediately. In a very serious voice, she looks Joseph right in the eyes and tells him, "You need to call Nico right now. Tell him I will be at the club with the rest of the Capo's of the crew. The club will be closed since it's a weekday, so we can hold the meeting there. Call Momo, Ron, Armand, and the rest of the Capo's. Tell them to be at the club in one hour, and not a minute late. This is an emergency."

Momo is still at the house since he brought Jenina's father over. He opens the door for Jenina and heads to pick up Big Ron. Jenina talks out loud, "I have to be awfully careful about how I run this meeting. This is my first meeting without Tony and Joseph. I need to watch what I say and stand my ground."

They arrive at the club. Nico is setting up the club's black chairs around a round table. Jenina hands him a twenty-dollar bill for coming in on his day off. The Capo's begin to arrive.

These guys are the big bosses, no street runners here. They consist of all Italians, some Sicilians and some Calabrians.

Chapter 15

"Unlikely Collaboration"

As the club begins to fill up with all the heads of all the crews they get drinks, sit down, and wait for the meeting to begin. In walks Jenina. She is dressed beautifully; her hair is flowing as usual. Beside her are Momo and Big Ron.

Out of the blue, Armand shouts, "Where is Joseph? We haven't got all day. We have crews to run. He knows this!"

Jenina replies, "Joseph's not coming. Show some respect Armand. Just because Tony's not here doesn't mean that people won't be dealt with. That disrespects Tony and Joseph. There is no weakness in either of them or especially not in me. I called this meeting."

The faces on the crew leaders dropped.

As mumbling is heard throughout the dining area, Jenina says, "Just stop! I'll explain everything. As you all know, Anthony's been in jail for the past 2 months. He cannot get any information out and no one's allowed to see him from the crew except for me.

"With that, I'm not running the crew but I am transferring the information that Anthony's given to me to you guys so you can keep the crew running smoothly.

"Now, we have a problem. We have a crew of guys from Chicago that are in New York. Some of our close friends cannot find them, so I have another idea. I have friends in the Black Mafia in Harlem that could possibly help us root the guys out because they're planning something against us. They want to try to take over the Calabrese family's territory, which belongs to us. But, because of Anthony being in jail, we haven't been able to close everything needed to set up in those areas, so just listen to me. These things are coming from Anthony and Joseph, but I am the speaker. Does anyone have a problem with that? Let me know now."

As she looks around the room, she sees that Armand is one of the only ones with a smirk on his face. She takes that into mental consideration but holds the thought.

She still must find out who is leaking information. She believes she has an idea who, especially when he's been found coming out of the hotel room of Olivia Calabrese.

Jenina speaks, "So in other words, with a show of hands, I would really like to see who is on board with this so we can move forward and protect our territory while Anthony is taking care of his business. Chicago believes we are weak. We have to let them know that there's no weakness even though Tony is in jail. If that means the unlikely collaboration between us and Harlem, then it has to be done. Does anyone have a problem with that?"

All 30 captains raised their hands. She sees the resistance in some, but she believes she has the votes of the Capos to move forward, besides Armand. As the mumbling and restlessness seems to calm down one of the heads of the Capos stands up, Guido Castellano.

Guido says, "We understand and respect Tony and what he needs to do. If you're speaking in honor of him and Joseph, we believe that the right thing to do is to listen, so our families don't fall apart. The Black Mafia is dangerous. They have their territory, we have ours. We settled that war a long time ago. We don't want to do anything to start that all over again."

Jenina replies, "Don't worry about that. They owe me and my family, so I will handle the matter delicately and not include the Scalia family, only myself."

Guido says, "I owe my loyalty to Tony. Whatever you say will be done."

Jenina replies, "Thanks. We have a lot of work to do. With that, this meeting is adjourned."

The mumbling begins again. As the Capos get up and they start to leave Jenina calls out to Guido and pulls him aside.

She says, "I see the loyalty in your eyes for Tony. Can you please do me a favor and keep your eyes and ears open for someone in this crew, right here in this room, that's resistant?"

Guido replies, "I got you, boss."

Jenina says, "I'm not the boss, just an advisor."

They all leave. Momo says to Jenina, "Great job, you handled yourself perfectly. I couldn't have done a better job myself."

Jenina says, "Thanks I just said what came to mind."

Now the hard work begins.

Chapter 16

"Infiltrated"

Leaving the club, Armand stomps his feet and jumps into his car. He is infuriated and slams the door. He needs to vent, so he heads straight to Olivia's. Distracted, he can't get her beautiful body out of his head.

But then he immediately bounces back to Jenina. He says to himself, "What a bitch. I have been with Tony for 8 whole years. Why would he move her up and not me?" He punches the steering wheel as hard as he can. "I deserve this more than anyone in that crew. I am the most loyal!"

Meanwhile, there is a black car behind him. This car has been following Armand since he left the club, but he hasn't noticed. It is Guido Castellano. Guido remembers what

Jenina said to him and noticed that Armand had that smirk on his face during the meeting, so he decided to follow him.

In his car, Armand is cursing up a storm.

Guido notices that Armand pulled up to Olivia's apartment. He knows he is the snake and keeps going.

Armand parks his car quickly and runs up to Olivia's, banging on the door. He is very upset.

She opens the door, "Armand, hey you, I wasn't expecting to see you here. Is everything okay?"

He runs into her room. Clearly something is bothering him, she has never seen him like this before.

Olivia calms Armand down. She gets him a drink and tells him, "Armand, baby, you need to relax. Tell me about your day and what happened to make you so livid."

Armand says to her, "Listen Olivia, I knew this day would come. We were right about Jenina. She said that we must listen to her. There's no way in hell I would ever listen to, number one, a female, number two, a negro woman.

"Tony must think we're crazy. I've been with him so many years and he's never given me the right to address the entire crew for any reason. This is a travesty! We cannot let this happen.

"I wonder if The Association knows what's going on. If not, they will soon. She is trying to show the crew that she has power. This isn't good! Something must be done!

"Then she had the nerve to down-right threaten me! If I had any negative thoughts or views on the way Tony and Joseph are handling this crew...The nerve of her! I've been here way longer than her.

"The things that Tony, this crew, and I have been through are epic. We are the second largest crew in New York. Out of the five families that reside here, I cannot get over this.

"Tony's got to get out of prison and get this thing straightened out or I'll do something about it."

After hearing all of this from Armand Olivia's head is spinning. The only thing she can say to him is, "We must be smarter than that. We have to work our way around this or Joseph will retaliate. If he finds out, I know he and my father were very close at one time, and I may have been young, but I remember some of the things that they used to say.

"Joseph was cold. He won't hesitate to put you in the back of a trunk if you're not loyal to him."

Armand rants. "The hell with him. He's an old washed-up man. With Tony in jail, someone who has helped run this crew for so many years should be running the crew. That's all I'm saying."

Olivia replies, "We must be smart or we'll both end up dead. Be careful with what you say and do now Armand. You must go back and act like you're on her side and stay calm until you find out everything, then we'll figure this all out together."

Chapter 17

"February 14ᵗʰ"

February 14, 1921, Tony sits alone in his cell. He is thinking about Jenina as usual. He is visualizing their life together. Alone in a beautiful house for a few years, then maybe a few Tony Jr.'s running around. He imagines how beautiful Jenina would look pregnant, and how great of a mother she will be someday.

In the middle of his daydream, a guard comes into his cell and grabs him. "Where am I going?" Tony asks.

The guard doesn't respond. He walks him outside. Tony hasn't been outside of The Tombs at 125 White Street in Lower Manhattan for a long time. He forgets what the fresh air smells like and the sound of horns blaring.

Another inmate says to Tony, "We're going to St. Augustine, Florida."

Tony knows exactly where he is going now – 167 San Marco Ave, St. Augustine, Florida, 41 miles south of Jacksonville. His trial is finally here. They get into this rickety, old, government owned plane. "Thank God we are flying," Tony says to himself.

He sleeps the entire time on the plane and wakes up to sunshine. "Let's do this," he says.

Three days later Tony is sitting in the court room. He sees Rusty Ford, the gas station attendant that witnessed the shooting. Rusty is 6'3, 250 pounds and wearing dirty denim overalls and a grease filled truckers' hat.

Tony says to himself, "Hopefully someone paid his dirty ass off."

Tony's a little nervous but the lawyer says to him, "Don't say a word. We got this covered."

The bailiff calls Rusty to the stand. He gets sworn in.

The opposing lawyer asked Rusty, "What happened in the gas station?"

Rusty says to him, "I heard the scuffling and then I looked around the corner and two men were fighting." He continued, "The man with the hat was fighting the other guy that was in the car." Rusty pointed at Tony and says, "Then the guy with the hat pulled a gun out on

Tony and then Tony pulled his gun. The scuffle ensued and then I heard a gun go off. The guy on the ground was bleeding. Tony ran to his car and drove off. There also was a woman in the car but I didn't get to see her. I just saw a woman's hat."

Since there wasn't anyone else around, the Judge had to go off of what Rusty said, that it was self-defense. Rusty also adds, "I heard the man pointing at Tony yelling at him asking why he was following them."

Also, in Tony's defense, his lawyer states, "I have documents that they were at the bungalow and

that the bungalow was ransacked." That's really the only evidence they had was Rusty and the documents from the bungalow association.

The judge states, "Now I'm going to my chambers, and I will come out with a decision." Since this was a judge lead trial and not a jury trial, they do this in case they try to bribe the jury.

During the recess Tony asked his lawyer, "What do we do now?" The lawyer says again, "Don't worry about it. It's all taken care of. How come everyone talks about the man with the hat? What does that mean?"

Tony replies, "Well almost everyone wears hats, but this hat was unique. It was tall, almost like a 10-gallon hat, but maybe 5 gallon."

Laughter ensues between Tony and the lawyer.

The lawyer says, "No one else has a hat like that. I've never seen it before."

Tony replies, "One of my associates owns a hat store and he's never seen it before. It's very unique."

A little bit of time goes by.

They hear the door open. The judge comes out. The bailiff yells, "All rise. On docket number 2212, prisoner number 1120, Anthony Ripina."

The judge says, "I would like to address the court that I have made my decision. You are being charged with first degree murder, leaving the scene of a crime, leaving the scene of a crime crossing multiple state lines, deadly assault, my decision is this: You are guilty on all counts but the murder charge has been changed to 3rd degree manslaughter. That carries a sentence of 3-5 years with time spent in the New York jail system. Including the time you have spent here, the decision is 3 years in the penitentiary. This will only be known by the people involved. No one else will know what jail you will be sent to. You will serve two and a half years. With that please detain the prisoner and take him away. Your time starts today, Anthony."

Tony has a look in his eyes like 'What just happened? Only two and a half years? This is why I love Joseph.' They take him away. He says to Vince, his lawyer, "Thank you so much Vince."

He replies, "I told you we would take care of you Tony. If it were anyone else, they would be getting at least 10 to 20. Stay well and be well. You'll be out in no time. I will notify Joseph that everything went well. If you didn't get any time, then things would have looked suspicious. With good behavior you could probably file in about 18 months. We're not going to appeal because it might make matters worse. Be well, God bless, and we'll take care of everything. Jenina is doing a good job standing up for you while you're away."

Tony replies, "That's the worst part about this. I miss her so much. Please tell her I love her, I miss her, and I will be good in prison to get out as soon as possible. Thank you."

He shakes Vince's hand. They handcuff Tony and take him away.

Chapter 18

"Overseas Delivery"

As Jenina returns to Joseph's house, she enters the front door and is greeted by Stephanie. Stephanie says, "Hey! How did everything go?" Jenina replies, "Everything went well I think, except for one person. Everyone else seemed to be on board." Stephanie says, "Let's go into the parlor, we have to talk. Do you want anything to eat or drink? Are you hungry?"

Jenina says, "No thank you Stephanie, not right now. I still have butterflies in my stomach from the meeting." Jenina heads into the parlor.

Stephanie says, "Sit down. I have something to talk to you about. Considering the things that you are involved in right now, you cannot have this baby here. I came up with a plan where you and I can go to Europe, actually, Paris."

Jenina says with excitement, "I can't believe it! Really? Paris? I've always wanted to go to Europe."

Stephanie says, "Don't you worry Jenina, it'll be no problem. I did want to mention something. I think your mother should be there, that would only be right. We can take her too."

Jenina says, "Wow. She would love that. Oh my God! Can my sister come too? My dad will be fine at his friend Trigger's house."

Stephanie replies, "I don't think that would be a problem at all."

Jenina says, "Well actually they don't know that I am pregnant yet. Thank goodness I'm carrying small."

Stephanie replies, "Well you only have 3 months to go. Tony's intending on getting out in 18 months, so we have to get a move on. Plus, there are things you need to do when you return. While things are calm around here, we should go."

Jenina is super excited. She cannot believe she's already been to Bermuda, now she's going to magical Paris. She's feeling as though being with Tony was the right thing to do. Ever since she met him, she has been experiencing things that she never could have imagined. Now she's including her family, which is all she's ever wanted.

What Jenina is doing is a little dangerous and risky, but she believes it's well worth it. She is not afraid of anything anymore. Every day she is growing stronger. There is one thing looming over her head. She can't stop thinking about the Armand and Olivia situation. It is really bothering her. She knows how brutal women can be so it's more Olivia than Armand.

The crew can handle him, but Jenina knows that in the near future she's going to have to deal with Olivia. With her raging hormones, she is not afraid of anyone at this point. She really needs to leave for a little while. This trip is the best thing for her right now. First of all, Jenina needs to explain to her mom that she's pregnant and why she never told her. Her parents may be upset but she knows her sister is going to be super excited.

Stephanie goes into the smoking room with Joseph and starts to plan this vacation. Her responsibility is to get things on track for four people.

They have connections to help get passports for black women because it is hard for black women to travel overseas. Joseph had to make some phone calls. The only thing Jenina has to do is to go with Big Ron and Momo to Trigger's house to give the mom, dad, and sister the good news.

She is so tired and going to head over to Tony's house, which is the house that they share next to Joseph and Stephanie. She is going to rest. She has no problem sleeping because she's protected by the guards that watch over the property.

Chapter 19

"The News"

Jenina wakes up at 6:43 AM, just in time for the sunrise. The sky is painted pink, purple, and a tint of blue. She prays to God that the day will turn out the way she wants it to. She has a good feeling because the sun is out today.

Jenina puts on her mother's favorite color dress and a beautiful pearl necklace. She is so excited to see them because it's been a while.

Jenina takes a walk over to Joseph's house to talk to Stephanie. Stephanie greets Jenina with a big smile, "Good morning sunshine. Everything is going to turn out great today. Don't worry about a thing."

Jenina replies, "Thank you Stephanie, I just want to get this

over with. I am excited to see my family."

Big Ron beeps the horn. Jenina gives Stephanie a hug and leaves.

As Big Ron and Jenina approach the house, Jenina is not feeling so well. It could be the car ride, her anxiety, or the baby. Jenina says to Big Ron, "Stay here. I will talk to Trigger."

Jenina heads into the house and is greeted by Trigger's girlfriend. "Jenina. We are so happy to see you. Your mom, dad, and sister are upstairs. I'll tell Trigger to come here first."

Trigger comes downstairs and expresses how happy he is to see her. Jenina says, "Trigger, can you please send someone outside to watch my car and my driver?"

Trigger replies, "No problem, I'll send a guard out immediately."

Syreeta hears Jenina's voice and runs downstairs. "Jenina? Is that you!"

Following right behind her is her mother and father. Syreeta jumps into Jenina's arms. Her father smiles and says, "To what do we owe this occasion?"

Her mother kisses her on the forehead, "How's my baby? I see you're wearing my favorite dress. That is such a great look on you."

Jenina replies, "I missed you guys so much. Mom, I need to talk to you."

The dad asks, "Is everything okay Jenina?"

Jenina says, "Yes, I just need to talk to mom privately. Can we go into the office?"

Jenina and her mother head into Trigger's office. Jenina hugs her mom and looks into her eyes and asks, "Mom, how would you like to go on a cruise?"

Her mother replies, "Jenina. What are you talking about? You know we can't afford to go on a cruise. I don't even have my own house right now."

Jenina says, "We don't need any money, the trip is all paid for."

The mom replies, "I told you before Jenina, this family does not take handouts."

Jenina says, "Joseph's wife, Stephanie, wants to go to Europe and wants company. I said that I wouldn't go without you and Syreeta."

Her mom replies, "What about your father? I can't leave your father."

Jenina says, "Our dad is strong. He is with his friend Trigger. They survived a war together. I'm sure they could survive a few months without you and Syreeta."

The mom asks, "A few months? Why so long?"

Jenina replies, "Can I tell you something without your judgment?"

Her mother replies, "What's wrong? I knew something was wrong. What is the matter?"

Jenina says, "Tony and I are engaged."

Her mother pulls her left hand and looks at the ring and says, "Tony said something to me when we were at the hospital about wanting to marry you. I didn't think he was telling the truth. To be honest Jenina, I didn't believe him. But I guess he is a man of his word, and I am happy to have him as a part of our family."

Jenina says, "Good, because there's going to be even another addition to our family."

Her mother replies, "What? What do you mean?"

Jenina puts her mom's hand on her stomach. Her mother's eyes light up, she asks, "I'm going to be a grandmother?"

Jenina with tears in her eyes nods her head yes.

Her mother yells, "Syreeta, Al, get in here right now!"

Syreeta and her father run into the office. "What's going on?", they ask.

The mom hugs her husband and says to him, "We're going to be grandparents!"

Syreeta jumps for joy and hugs Jenina.

Jenina says, "Not too hard sis."

The mom says to Syreeta, "I have another surprise. Me, you, Jenina, and Stephanie Scalia are going on a trip."

Jenina cuts in, "Guess where we are going? Paris! I've heard they have great hospitals there. I can't wait to introduce you to Stephanie. She is wonderful. I just wanted to let y'all know that I need you to be there with me and have your blessing. But right now, I have to leave. We don't want the car out front for very long. We are leaving for the trip in 2 days, so pack your bags! We will send a car to bring you both to Joseph's house."

Her dad replies, "Don't worry about me girls. I'll be fine with Trigger until you get back. There is a lot of protection around. I feel completely safe."

Jenina gives hugs all around and leaves.

Chapter 20

"Departure"

As Jenina leaves triggers home she feels a bit of sadness because of leaving her father but she knows he'll be okay because trigger will always protect him. So, they head to the Scalia mansion where Jenina has things to think about and to get ready to leave for their trip. But what's really on her mind is the relationship between Olivia and Armand she knows this could bring a whole heap of trouble to the family. But she's trying to stay positive because there's a lot riding on this trip basically the baby and her mental stability.

She only has two days to try to figure out how she's going to handle these things especially when she returns because she'll have the baby and her thinking will have to be different. She knows this.

Finally, the day has come where they're leaving for Paris. It's a joyful day because the lowest women never would believe that they will be going to Europe. This is something that rarely happens with black women in the twenties due to racial injustice, so they feel they're very lucky to have known the Scalia family.

Momo pulls up in the car with Eloise and Syreeta. They both jumped out of the car hugging and kissing Jenina so joyfully ready to go to Europe and thanking Stephanie and Joseph for the opportunity to leave the country, which may have never happened if they didn't pull strings for them.

They packed their things in the car and they're off to the New York Harbor to depart to Europe. It's a busy port. Basically, the busiest port in the United States at that time connecting the United States with Europe with shipping of all sorts of goods.

They arrive to the port. It's very busy. The porter takes their baggage, and they board the "RMS Aquitania" it's a large vessel, very overcoming to the ladies and beautiful.

Once they arrive to their cabin, Jenina says, "I'm very tired. I'm gonna take a nap."

Eloise replies, "I understand. I know that feeling!"

So, she lays down. The other women take a walk to the deck. They have a pretty long ride to La Havre port then a three-hour train ride to Paris. It's a very long but exciting trip.

The Lewis ladies are being treated like queens, something that Eloise never thought would happen to her being raised in the poverty-stricken part of Harlem, so she is totally amazed. Most black women would never see Europe throughout the course of their lifetime, only high-profile blacks like entertainers, sport's figures and dignitaries would enjoy the luxury of taking this trip.

La Havre is a city on the northern side of Europe. It's very rustic in appearance but beautiful.

The trip is long and grueling but, in the long run, they're all enjoying themselves.

As they reach the port of la Havre, they're getting very excited because they're close to reaching Paris. It's only a couple hours ride away by train.

They arrive in their hostel in Paris. It's a lovely place full of life and history. The ladies enjoy their time in Paris.

Meanwhile in New York, trouble is brewing with the Chicago mob plotting against Joseph and his crew.

Chapter 21

"Exceeding Expectations"

Momo and Big Ron have big shoes to fill as Tony comes near the end of his time spending in jail and Jenina and Stephanie's trip comes to an end.

The protection that they're giving Joseph against the impending attack from Chicago is going well but one gloomy night, shots rang out at the Scalia mansion, as expected. All hands-on deck as an attack on Joseph's home becomes a reality.

Momo and Big Ron gather up the men as they scurry around to see where the shots are coming from. It seems there is multiple shooters coming from a distance.

They scatter around looking for their enemies, but no one is to be found.

Big Ron realizes what direction the shots are coming from and is heading in that direction.

Momo runs upstairs to check on Joseph when he opens Joseph's door, he's shocked to see that Joseph got hit! A sniper bullet comes right through the window and hits Joseph in the back. He began yelling, "Joseph! Joseph! are you okay?"

Joseph speaks quietly, "I'm okay."

Momo replies, "Yes you are you're going to be fine." Momo yells out, "Someone call the doctor!"

Geo replies, "He's on the way!"

Meanwhile, Big Ron approaches the house dragging a bleeding ruffed up man towards the home yelling, "I caught one!"

Momo tells Geo to look after Joseph till the doc arrives while he helps Ron get the man into the basement.

Big Ron and Momo interrogate the man while he's strapped to a chair and beat him until he finally rats on the Chicago boss. This is the last straw when Jenina gets back.

"We're gonna end this!" says Momo.

"Also, there is a rat still in our organization," states Big Ron, "And I think I know who it is. I'll deal with that ASAP. He's most likely the reason they know where Joseph's home is.

Meanwhile, in Paris the other girls are out as Jenina is having contractions. She is afraid and doesn't know what to do. Just as they got closer Mom and Stephanie walk through the door.

Mom yells out as she dropped her bags and says, "You ok?"

Jenina replies, "I think it's time."

Stephanie leaps into action gathering blankets, towels, and warm water.

Mom says, "Be calm, child. This isn't the first baby I helped deliver. There was a time when negro women couldn't go to the hospital to deliver."

Stephanie and Eloise work together to deliver Tony and Jenina's beautiful baby girl.

"Thank you both so much," Jenina says.

"No need to thank us, thank you! You made us both grandparents!!" Stephanie says playfully.

"Anthony and Joseph will be so happy!" says Mom.

Stephanie replies, "Let's not get too comfortable. We still have to go to the hospital to get her checked out, the both of them. Do you know what her name will be?"

Jenina replies, "Yes. I think that I will combine our names. Her name will be Antonina."

They both love the name. Mom and Stephanie and tell her how cute that is.

Little do they know, back in New York, the doctor speaks to Big Ron stating that Joseph is in bad shape. The bullet was lodged in his back. He was trying to leave the room when the bullet came through the window. His lung was punctured, and the doctor said it cannot be removed. They don't know how much longer he has to live.

Big Ron and Momo are furious. They're ready to move on Chicago without permission from Jenina but they know that the best thing is to wait until she returns and see what she wants to do and how she wants to do it.

The time has come for the girls to return to New York. They have a long grueling trip back but they're all happy and Antonina is doing fine.

In the meantime, in New York, they're trying to make Joseph as comfortable as possible hoping and praying that he hangs on long enough to see his wife again. Big Ron and Momo are getting very edgy knowing that the rest of those men got away. But at least now they know where they came from. This is going to be very hard for them to tell Stephanie because it was on their watch.

The day has come for Momo and Big Ron to pick the girls up. They approach the dock they see a baby in Jenina's arms. The women approach Big Ron and Momo giving hugs.

Momo says, "Whose baby is this?"

Stephanie replies, "It's Tony's baby."

Laughter and smiles are on everyone's face but then a sadness comes over Momo's face.

Stephanie replies, "What's wrong?"

Momo says, "We'll talk when we get home."

Stephanie replies, "Is everything okay?"

Momo says, "Not really."

The girls enter the car. Everyone has a plain look on their face. The happiness has gone away because Stephanie doesn't feel like everything is going to be okay.

They approach the Scalia mansion the help is all outside with a somber look on their faces.

The maid Elma says, "Welcome back everyone! what a beautiful baby!"

Stephanie replies, "She is! her name is Antonina. It's Jenina and Anthony's baby, my grandchild."

Stephanie and Jenina to come right upstairs and bring the baby. As the door opens to the bedroom, Stephanie runs in and sees Joseph laying in the bed looking very sickly. She runs to the bed and hugs Joseph and ask, "Are you okay my dear? I miss you so much!"

Joseph replies, "I love you, too. I had a stroke of bad luck. I'm hit in the back and the bullet cannot be removed. I'm sorry."

Stephanie replies, "No, I'm sorry I wasn't here for you."

Joseph says, "I'm glad you weren't here. There were bullets everywhere. I love you so much.

"Jenina who are you holding in your arms?"

Jenina replies, "Your grandchild. This is Anthony's baby."

A smile comes over his face he says, "I'm glad I'm here to see this. I don't know how much longer I can hang on. I wish Tony was here. She is just so beautiful! what is her name?"

Jenina replies, "It is Anthony's name and my name together. her name is Antonina."

Joseph replies, "What a beautiful name for my granddaughter and it sounds Italian!" A smile comes over his face.

Jenina replies, "I realize that, too. I love it! Now down to business, who did this to you?"

Joseph replies, "Talk to Big Ron and Momo. They have the details. Just do me a favor. You're a new mom, now. Please, be careful."

Jenina says, "I will. I understand."

Big Ron Momo and Jenina go into The Parlor and shut the door.

Jenina asks, "Who the hell did this? Whoever it is they're going to pay dearly!"

Momo replies, "They were from the Chicago faction. They want control of the

Calabrese family territory which belongs to the five families of New York and not Chicago.

Jenina replies, "No matter what we have to end this! Get everyone together. We're going to pay them a little visit for the last time."

They gather up the men and have a Capo sit down. Together, they plan the attack on Chicago which is very dangerous because they're going into the state of Illinois and really don't know how many soldiers await them. They will have to plan a sneak attack. Since Jenina is very smart, Big Ron and Momo have confidence that she knows what she's doing.

Chapter 22

"Epilogue"

Tony's getting out soon and he has a new baby, but his father is dying. She knows that having a baby will make him happy but will be overshadowed by the death of his father. Tony cannot be totally happy. What Jenina was feeling all along. ever since she started falling in love with Tony, is to get him out of this business because she doesn't want him to wind up with a bullet in his back someday. So, she knows what she must do. She must end this so they can peacefully walk away from this terrible business. It's basically coming to an end anyway because prohibition is on its way out. Joseph will not have his men sell drugs, only gambling, booze, and loansharking.

Stephanie is by Joseph side as he peacefully passes away. This day is a somber day for he was a good man but stern. This is the things that he taught Anthony to be. The household has a sadness over it. He will be truly missed.

Tony has one month before he gets out. The problem is, he won't be able to attend the funeral because of the simple fact that he is an undocumented stepchild of Joseph and Stephanie. He was never officially adopted. It's sad to everyone because he won't be able to say goodbye to his dad from which he's known since he was 12 years old.

The following week, the funeral takes place. There are dignitaries from all over whom Joseph dealt with. Police officers, captains, judges, lawyers, and even the mayor shows up at his huge funeral letting Stephanie know that Joseph will be truly missed. Jenina is very sad especially for Tony who he has looked up to for many years. Her blood is boiling over this.

At this point, Jenina is very tired from having the baby, the long trip home, taking care of problem from Chicago. Also, the funeral took a lot from her. She needs peace and quiet. She needs to take a break soon. Tony will be coming home, and she needs to have her sanity. So, when she returns to the Scalia home a couple days later, she goes to her and Tony's beautiful home right next door. She brings Antonina there with her. She has a beautiful Nursery that they made just for her. Her and the baby lay down for a good night's rest.

Anthony's release is today and Jenina is getting excited that he's being transported back to NY from an undisclosed prison location. She's getting dolled up for him, wearing his favorite blue dress and dressing Antonina the same. She hears Momo blow. The horn. It's time to go. She's having butterflies fluttering in her stomach from nervousness.

As they pull up to the detention center, Momo says, "Tony is gonna be happy about the baby."

Jenina replies, "I know, but his heart will be crushed about his dad."

The gate opens. It's Tony!

Momo gets out of the car and walks towards the center to greet him.

Momo says, "Welcome home, boss!"

Tony replies, "OMG! My good friend! Good to see you! Where's Jenina?"

"In the car, boss. She has a little surprise for you!"

Tony scurries towards the car. As he approaches, he sees something on her lap.

She opens the door and carefully gets out.

He sees the folded blanket and stops in his tracks, drops his bag. Tears start rolling down his face. He hugs them both without even seeing the baby yet. He gives Jenina a big, long kiss and then starts to unravel the blanket. He sees his beautiful baby, with hazel eyes, long straight black hair, and very light skin. He cries out, "She is absolutely gorgeous!!"

Tony says, "She looks just like her mother, beautiful."

Jenina replies, "She looks like you. Also, that's why her name is Antonina."

Tony can't control himself.

Momo says, "Let's get away from this God forsaken place."

Tony says, "I can't wait to see my parents! I bet they are happy grandparents!"

With sadness in her eyes, she replies, "We'll talk when we get there. Here, Tony, hold your daughter on the way home.

Tony says, "Gladly! I want to bond with her more than anything. Is everything ok at home?"

Jenina says, "we'll talk when we get there. OK?"

As their approach to Scalia mansion, Tony sees Stephanie and all the help on the step waiting for him. He steps out as Stephanie approaches him with a somber look on her face. She hugs him and starts crying saying, "Your dad! Your dad! I really miss your dad!"

Tony starts to tear up. "I know, Mom. I'm sorry I wasn't here to say goodbye. He saved me. If it wasn't for him, I most likely would not be here right now. I'm going to get those bastards that did this to him."

Stephanie replies, "When you get settled, have a talk with Jenina. She'll explain everything."

Tony replies, "What do you mean, mom?"

As Jenina brings the baby inside, Tony asks her, "What did she mean by that?"

Jenina replies, "Just come inside and we'll talk as soon as I settle down the baby. We have nothing to worry about anymore."

Tony and Jenina go into the Parlor. She's explaining to him how everything happened. He's so shocked that she would take a chance on her and the baby's life to clean up a mess. He was upset but happy that she made it through everything with Momo and Big Ron behind her.

Tony says, "This house. My dad's death. My mother's sadness is hard to bear. We need a change. There is nothing stopping us from leaving this place. I'll notify the Association that I'm turning the entire business over to Ron and Momo. We never need to worry about money, ever. They deserve all this. They helped build this powerful empire. I love them both like brothers. Their loyalty to me and my dad is unbelievably true. So, let's tell Mom and your family we're moving to lovely Bermuda."

Jenina jumps for joy and replies, "I never wanted to leave there anyways! I love you, Tony! Perfect place for our daughter to be raised!!"

"Agreed!" Tony replies.

Jenina leaves to give the good news to the family. Tony, Big Ron, and Momo go to the parlor. Tony closes the door. Tony begins to explain what's going on. Ron and Momo are very pleased that the couple will be getting away from all this mess and raising their daughter in a peaceful place. They're also very thankful that Tony is turning the business over to them. They hug and toast glasses to their new venture together. They also say they will let Tony know everything will be okay and they will stay in touch.

Tony thinks this is a great idea being as though Momo is a bruiser and Big Ron is the brains.

Jenina and her family, except her dad, are in the living room celebrating the move of their family to such a beautiful place. Jenina says, "I can't wait to tell Dad. He'll be so happy! I wanna tell him personally!"

Jenina catches Momo, Ron, and Tony coming out of the parlor laughing. She says, "Momo, can you please take me to get my dad?"

Momo replies, "No problem, ma'am!"

They arrive at Triggers home. Jenina knocks and Triggers girlfriend answers.

"Hey! Long time no see!" she says. "Your dad is eating lunch on the terrace with Trigger. Follow me."

Excited, Jenina sees her dad. They rush to each other's arms! Alexander hugs Jenina tightly and says, I'm so happy my oldest is ok! It's been so long. How is Mom and Syreeta?"

Jenina replies, "I'm fine, Dad. Everyone is OK. I have so much good news to tell you! First, finish your lunch. Then, gather all your things. We're taking a one-way trip! We're finally at peace!"

"Whatever do you mean, child?" asks Alexander.

"Let's just say, the city is clean! It only took guts and brains. I'll explain later."

Jenina thanks Trigger for all his help and tells him his territory is safe and protected by the Scalia family from outside interference. She also leaves fifty thousand dollars on his table knowing he would never accept anything for protecting his close friend. On the way back to the Scalia home, Jenina and her dad got reacquainted from being away so long.

As they approach the home, Jenina says "Dad, as we walk in, close your eyes."

He replies, "But why?"

"I have a big suprise for you."

They walk in and Jenina tells her dad to outstretch his arms with eyes closed. They place Antonina in his arms.

Jenina says, "Open your eyes to the most beautiful sight you'll ever see."

Alexander opens his eyes and says, "Who am I holding?"

Jenina replies, "It's your grandchild."

Alexander squeezes the baby tight with tears in his eyes. He says, "What's her name?"

"Antonina. This is the reason I've been away so long. Tony and I have a child and I didn't know how you would take it.

They all hug around the baby with tears flowing. Jenina explains about Joseph's death, eliminating the potential threat to the family, and about the home and land they purchased in Bermuda. Tony has been busy since being home tying loose ends so everything runs smoothly, especially with the Association; they also gave their condolences and blessings for the future and in hopes for great business dealings with Momo and Big Ron.

Tony finally comes out of the parlor slightly frazzled.

Alexander walks over to him and says, "I'm so sorry. I had you plugged wrong. I apologize."

Mom also says, "I apologize for being so hard on y'all because of what I've been through."

Tony replies, "No need. I would have acted the same way about my daughter if it was me."

They shake hands.

Alexander says, "Welcome to the family. You're a good man."

Tony says, "As soon as we get settled there, we're getting married, so it'll be official."

He hugs Jenina with baby in hand. "I took care of everything. We're leaving in two days. I love you all! Relax tomorrow. We'll say goodbye to my dad and visit the mausoleum."

As the family gathers around the memorial for Joseph and say prayers for him it's a somber feeling amongst them. Tony especially, because he couldn't attend the funeral. So, everyone let Tony and his dad have time together.

After some time alone talking to his dad, he asked to hold Antonina while he was praying for his father, vowing to make her life peaceful and safe as possible. He found some sense of peace knowing he lived to see his only grandchild.

The time has come to leave. Tony hugs Jenina, his mom, and the baby with tears in his eyes sorrowful saying, "I'm gonna miss that sweet old man. He took me in when I had nothing and no one in this world could ever say that he wasn't my dad. He will forever be in my heart."

After this very sorrowful moment they return home Stephanie and Eloise cook dinner. They're leaving in the morning so everyone's quite sad but packing, knowing that there will be a better and safe life ahead of them.

As day breaks, everyone is eating breakfast contemplating the journey ahead. Momo and Big Ron are speaking to the captains about moving forward with the Scalia Family business. Also, they are saying their goodbyes to everyone and safe journey.

The men are helping them pack the car giving hugs and thanks all around. Finally, they're on the way to the port.

As they are leaving, Anthony says, "I'm gonna miss this place all the glitz and glamor but the peacefulness ahead is worth more than this"

jenina concurs.

They reach the port. People are boarding. Tony says, Let's get going. We have different cabins to sort out and we want to be comfortable before we set sail. They say their goodbyes to Momo and big Ron and board this gigantic ship. The porter takes their luggage, and they board the ship. Alexander cannot believe how large the ship is. He's never been on board an ocean liner before.

"It's beautiful!" he says.

Jenina says, "This is my third time on a ship, and this is my second time to Bermuda. it's so beautiful there."

Her dad says, "You're blessed, child!"

They settle in nicely to their cabins carefully watching the baby for any signs of sickness due to the choppy water.

As they awake on day two, the ocean is very angry the waves are getting higher and higher the family is starting to get concerned about this trip.

While looking out the porthole, Jenina says, "It seems like a storm is brewing."

Tony replies, "It's gonna be OK. We'll just ride it out. This is a gigantic ship. It can hold its own."

But the seas got worse. The sky turns to black in the middle of the day. Tony asks everyone to huddle up in one cabin together. It seems like the world is against this one ship and it isn't being controlled by the captain anymore. Everyone is getting scared. All they can hear is people screaming and running around violently.

Then they hear a knock at the door with a voice saying, "Is anyone in there? Women, children and old folks first! Everyone is to meet on the deck. We must abort the ship. We have hit reef and we're losing buoyancy. We hit reef! We hit reef! Everyone to the deck!"

So, Tony tries to keep everyone calm. They leave the cabin and head for the deck. As they arrive, there is so much confusion and dropping rafts into the water. It's a chaotic scene but Tony must keep his cool. He wants to send Stephanie, Jenina's mom, dad, sister, the baby and Jenina in the first ones going into the water.

Jenina does not want to go. She wants to stay with Tony and have the baby safe, but she will not leave him. Jenina says, "I love you, Tony, and I will stay with you forever. I meant that. I will not leave you here. I'll wait with you for the other raft boats to be lowered but let's put them on the raft so we know they will be safe."

Tony replies, "No way! Get in the boat!"

Jenina says, "I will not! I will stay with you till the end. I love you."

Tony knows at this moment how much he means to her, but the life of their baby means more to them than life itself.

She feels like life without Tony isn't life at all. Not being selfish about the baby but she knows it's the best chance for survival for the baby and if they make it, she will be very well taken care of.

As the raft lowers everyone is crying. The baby is wrapped in a blanket held by Eloise. They hear the baby's cries. It's heart breaking for them not knowing if they will see her grow but they know she'll be in good hands.

The raft reaches the water and they started drifting away. As they grew further away in the darkness of the violent sea, they can see the silhouette of Tony and Jenina hugging and kissing on the deck. The parents in the raft are praying for their safe return to Bermuda and there are enough boats to rescue them from the sinking ship.

As the ship is out of sight, Syreeta is holding Antonia she is saying to her, "No matter what happens, I will let the world know what a strong, smart woman your mother is and tell the story of how her as a Mulatto became the only legitimate 'Queen of New York'"

www.ingramcontent.com/pod-product-compliance
Lightning Source LLC
Chambersburg PA
CBHW071346130726
47996CB00002B/830